AF292334

For Lucia and Bethan,
my bluebirds
H.D.

For Tom,
with love
D.S.

Published in the UK by Alison Green Books, 2025
An imprint of Scholastic
1 London Bridge, London SE1 9BG
Scholastic Ireland, 89E Lagan Road,
Dublin Industrial Estate, Glasnevin, Dublin D11 HP5F
www.scholastic.co.uk
Designed by Zoë Tucker

Text copyright © Helen Docherty, 2025
Illustrations copyright © Daniela Sosa, 2025

The right of Helen Docherty and Daniela Sosa to be identified as the
Author and Illustrator of this Work has been asserted by them under the
Copyright, Designs and Patents Act, 1988.

HB ISBN: 978 0 702315 20 6
PB ISBN: 978 0 702315 21 3

All rights reserved
Printed in China

Paper made from wood grown in responsible
and other controlled forest resources.

1 3 5 7 9 10 8 6 4 2

All the Ways I Love You

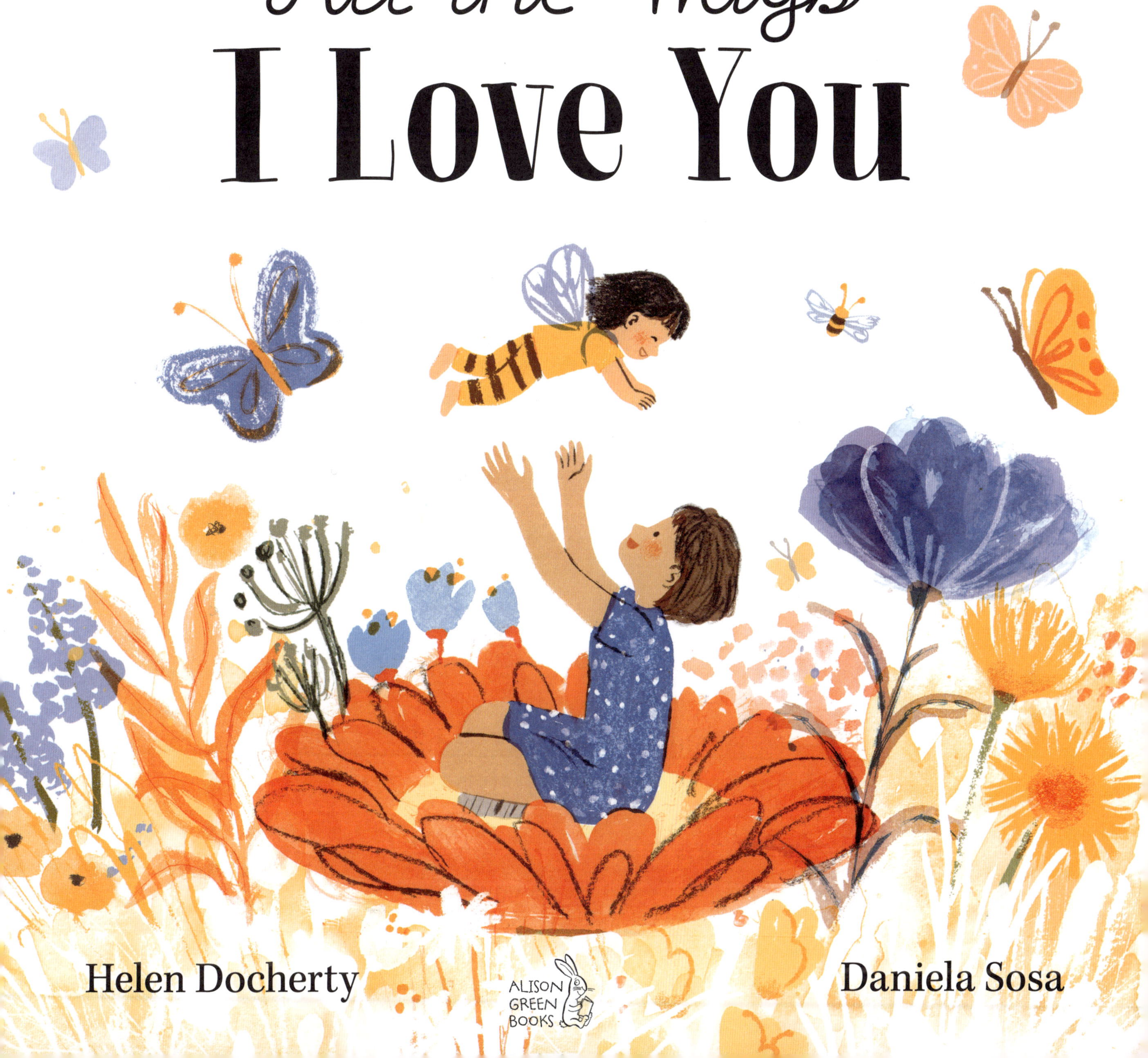

Helen Docherty

Daniela Sosa

If you were a **rainbow**,
I would be the sky.
I'd feed you lots of sun and rain
To keep you **shining high**.

If you were a garden snail,
I would be your shell.
I'd **shelter** you from any harm
And keep you safe and well.

If you were a firework,
I would be a spark.
I'd help you launch into the sky,
Blazing through the dark.

If you were an acorn,

I would be the earth.

I'd nourish and encourage you
For all that I was worth.

If you were a honey bee,
I would be a flower.
I'd let you drink my nectar
And fill you with my **power**.

If you were a dolphin,
I would be a wave.

I'd roll and dive and leap with you
Through the ocean brave.

If you were a monkey,
I would be a vine.

I'd help you swing from tree to tree;
I'd be your safety line.

If you were a crocodile,

I'd be an alligator.

We'd **laugh** and chat
and joke a while,

And then say:
"See you later!"

If you were a little cloud,
I would be the breeze.
I'd take you on a journey

Over cities, hills and trees.

If you were a set of pens,
I would be your ink.
Together we would **paint the world**
In blue and brown and pink.

If you were a bluebird,
I would be your nest.
I'd be a home to welcome you;
A place where you could rest.

If you were a baby,
This **promise** I would keep:
I'd rock you gently in my arms
Until you fell asleep.